TOP
SECRET

Copyright © 2018 by Clavis Publishing Inc., New York

First published as *Jan Politieman* in Belgium and Holland by Clavis Uitgeverij, Hasselt—Amsterdam, 2016
English translation from the Dutch by Clavis Publishing Inc., New York

Visit us on the Web at www.clavisbooks.com.

Officer Pete written and illustrated by Ruth Wielockx

ISBN 978-1-60537-378-2 (hardback edition)
ISBN 978-1-60537-398-0 (paperback edition)

This book was printed in April 2018 at Publikum d.o.o., Slavka Rodica 6, Belgrade, Serbia.

First Edition
10 9 8 7 6 5 4 3 2 1

Ruth Wielockx

OFFICER PETE

Dallas Public Library

Clavis

NEW YORK

Welcome to the police academy! **OFFICER PETE** works here.
Do you see those shiny motorcycles and police cars with flashing
blue lights? And the helicopter on the roof?

Behind the police station is the field where officers can play exercise to stay fit. And a field for the police horses. Can you find Officer Pete? He is training his tracker dog, **Sniffer**.

Today **OFFICER PETE** is on an important mission.
The chief asked him to take a letter
to the post office. It says **TOP SECRET** in big
black letters on the envelope.

Pete puts the letter safely in his pocket and heads out.
Hey, what's happening?
"My cap!" **OFFICER PETE** calls out.
"Someone stole my cap! **Stop thief!**"

"He went that way," says Officer Rob.
Pete doesn't hesitate. He jumps on a police motorcycle and drives off super-fast.
He'll catch that thief!

OFFICER PETE searches the neighborhood
on his motorcycle.
But he doesn't see the thief.
So he goes back to get some help . . . .

"Find the thief, **Sniffer**! Go!"
Sniffer immediately finds a trail.

Pete runs after his dog.
He can hardly keep up!
Where is **Sniffer** heading?

Sniffer dashes to the bakery.

"Police!" Pete says, and he shows his badge to the baker.

"I'm investigating the case of the stolen police cap."

The baker shakes his head. "No police caps here. Nothing but cakes and pies!"

Pete looks around the bakery and nods. "Thanks anyway," he says with a wave goodbye.

"We'll find the thief," **OFFICER PETE** says.
"Come on, **Sniffer**, let's go find my hat!"

Pete and **Sniffer** drive in a patrol car.
Suddenly Pete sees just the place.

There! In that shop window!

"Good afternoon! Police," Pete introduces himself.
"I'm investigating the case of the stolen police cap."
"Hmm. I have all sorts of hats and caps here, but unfortunately no police cap,"
the salesgirl says. The salesgirl was right; there is no police cap here.

"I'll never find my cap!" Pete moans.

Just then **OFFICER PETE** hears a parade going by.
"That's where we have to go, **Sniffer**!" Pete calls out.
"Maybe the thief is at the parade."

It's very busy at the market square!
Pete is undercover. He doesn't want the thief to notice him.
He carefully looks around. No thief. No police cap.

Where did his cap go?

OFFICER PETE and **Sniffer** jump in the police helicopter, because a real search operation is done from the sky. Pete searches the whole town with the searchlight, looking for the thief and his stolen cap.

Pete has tried everything: a chase,
a search with his tracker dog,
an interrogation, an undercover operation,
and even a search from the sky . . . and he *still*
didn't catch the thief! Maybe he'll never find the stolen cap.

Hey, what's that rustling in his pocket?
Oh boy . . . the secret letter!
He'd forgotten all about it!
As if his day wasn't bad enough.

Pete sighs. Then he hears a **beeping** sound.
His beeper! That means there is an urgent matter.

OFFICER PETE hurries to the chief's office.
His cap is sitting right there on the desk!

Pete doesn't understand. Why was his cap stolen and why was it there now?
The chief superintendent laughs very loudly:
"We borrowed your police cap so you would be able to wear . . ."

"...this **party hat!**"

Officer Pete was so busy today
that he forgot about his own birthday!

"Happy birthday to you! Happy birthday to you!" the other officers sing.
Pete gets a new police bike, and there are balloons and a delicious cake.
What a lovely surprise!

And the secret letter?
It's the nicest birthday card Pete has ever seen!